BEFORE
FINDING
FAMOUS

THE MAGIC JOURNAL

Alexis Anique

1

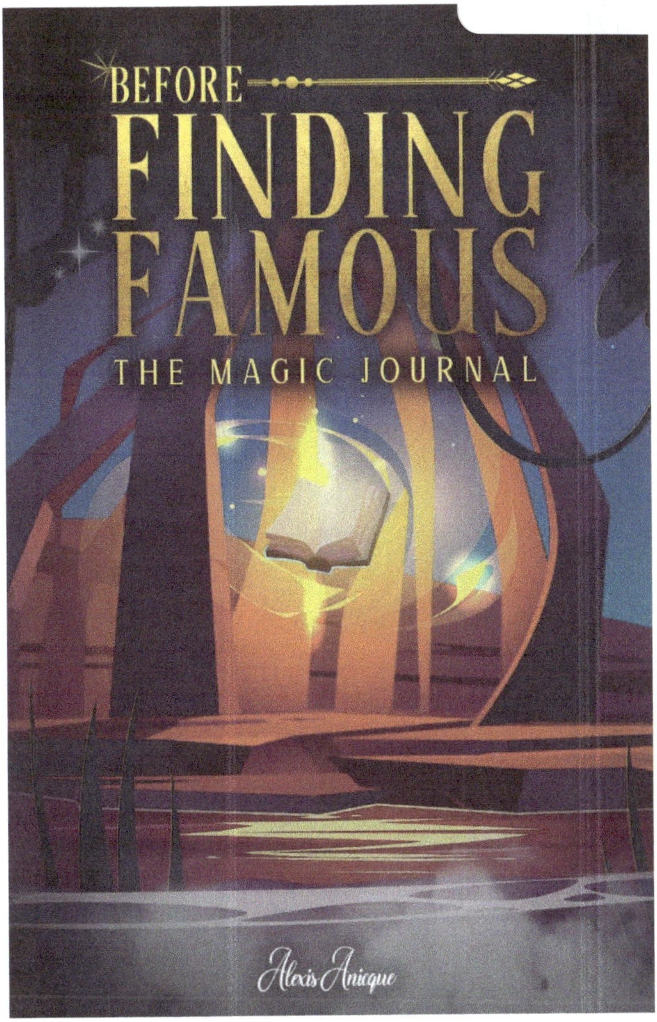

Before Finding Famous

The Magic Journal

Check out the Famous Adventure Series

Book One

Finding Famous

Book Two

Famous Destiny; The Monster in the Forest

Book Three

The Famous Christmas Memory; The Pumpkin Bread Recipe Fiasco

https://alexisanicque.com/

For questions regarding this book including quality or bulk purchase please contact at AlexisAnicque@gmail.com

Table of Contents

Prologue

Chapter 1 – Happy to Not be Normal

Chapter 2 – The Map

Chapter 3 – Who Was That?

Chapter 4 – The First Farmer's Market

Chapter 5 – The "Awake" Dream

Chapter 6 – The Knock

Chapter 7 – The Compass

Chapter 8 – The Cheapest Option

Chapter 9 – The Ferry

Chapter 10 – The Journal

Author Links

About the Author

Prologue

The long-awaited prequel to the Famous Adventure
Series in this mysterious magical tale that leads
Dar to the beginning, where it all started, the path
she must follow to find Famous.

Chapter One – Happy to Not be Normal

"What just happened?" Dar screamed to her mother as the dust cleared and her vision came back. She stood in the dimly lit shop with tables of odds and ends and racks of clothes hanging. A table had something glowing; she tried to see what it was, but things were beginning to blur. She was trying to focus and regain her memory of how she had gotten there. The last memory she had was her and her mom walking back to the hostel. "Mom?" Glancing in the darkness, she called out again and again. "Mom?"

Weeks earlier...

Dar Alegria had felt different for most of her life. She had never been like other children. Their family had always been unusual. A strange family with odd traditions, even when it came to naming their children, often waiting to see what their special characteristics were to find a fitting name. Dar's name is Spanish for "give joy"; a name her mother said fit her to a tee. She did give joy. Her very presence made others happy.

Dar's dark hair flowed past her shoulders but was normally pulled up in a ponytail. She wasn't especially interested in trivial things like make-up, fancy clothes, or materialistic belongings.

Dar's mother was named Luminous, Lumi for short, and she was born a true gypsy at heart. Lumi came from a long line of mystics, psychics, readers, and dreamers.

Dar was special, unlike many of the others, but she really didn't have dreams or mystical powers like the family she was born into. At least, she didn't believe she did. Although it was not apparent to her, it was obvious to the others: she radiated joy. It wasn't a quality Dar thought to be magical, but Lumi had told her many times throughout her life that one day, she would understand how powerful she really was.

As a child, Dar flowed through life, fluttered really, like a butterfly or a bird. Although she lived in the real world, she lived in a magical world as well. A joyous life of fun and travel with her mother. They lived a life of gypsies in the eyes of most. Her mother took her on many adventures.

Most of her life seemed far from normal to the outsider looking in. And they would be right. Her life was far from normal. One thing in particular was the fact that her dad was from another country. Her mom had gone to a summer internship program after college abroad, and it was here she met Dar's father.

Dar believed her parents were still very much in love; however, neither of her parents wanted to permanently move countries and Lumi wasn't much for a normal white picket fence lifestyle. They spent one month a year as a family. Of course, she spoke with him all the time. It wasn't until Dar went to school, which was a short-lived experience, that she found out that her family's lifestyle was not normal.

School was not Dar's cup of tea, and it wasn't long before she began taking her lessons at home. This worked well for Lumi. The short time Dar was in school, Lumi had trouble staying and working one place.

Lumi was a finder of lost things or people. Many called her a psychic detective, but neither Lumi nor Dar liked that title. A lot of what she found took investigative skills, determination, and travel.

Most of her work had come by word of mouth until a wealthy museum investor had hired her to find an artifact. The reward was substantially more than she had ever made for one job, which is she decided to begin spending more time looking for artifacts for historical societies.

She would spend hours at the library with Dar looking for new leads of missing artifacts, finding out who wanted them and how much she could earn if she found them.

This helped her to earn enough money. Sometimes one artifact could pay her bills for a year.

They lived a meager lifestyle, not that Dar knew that either. She thought she had the best life ever. Dar had been to more places than anyone she had ever met. Every day was an adventure. Her life was about experiences and that made her feel like the richest person alive. She was happy to not be normal.

Chapter Two – The Map

One day, Dar's mother came to her room and told her to pack only what she could carry. They were to embark on a journey. Dar asked where they were going. Lumi smiled, "I'm not sure yet. I only know we must go and find something. Although I am not yet sure what that something is, I am sure it will lead you to many fantastic adventures. It came to me in a dream many times over the years and the time has come to go find it."

Lumi had spent Dar's life taking her from place to place to look for things, so this was not unusual, but not knowing what she was looking for or where to start looking certainly was. They spent the day talking about where they should start looking. That night they even threw darts at their map that hung on their adventure wall, laughing and laughing.

Their adventure wall consisted of a large very detailed map which covered more than half of the wall. The map was surrounded by pictures of the two of them together on some kind of adventure in every place they had visited: white water rafting in the Canadian Rockies, ziplining in Costa Rica, riding a camel through the Saharan desert, and many more pictures full of grand adventures.

They continued to throw darts and laugh until they realized the darts had stuck in nearly the same area each and every time. Both knew it couldn't possibly be a coincidence. They each tried throwing another dart standing from different angles with the same result.

They each tried over and over to hit a different spot on the map, even trying with their eyes closed, but all darts landed in the same area. This was a place they had never been. They knew this to be true because each time they had gone somewhere, they would highlight the area on the map as soon as they returned home. It was Dar's favorite thing to do. She would often talk of the day when the entire map would be covered in yellow. This area was one of the few not yet highlighted.

They left that day and began the trek. Lumi had said they were looking for a market with loads of tables selling bits of everything. "So we're looking for a flea market?" Dar teased. Lumi just laughed it off knowing her time was limited with her. Dar was growing up and would go on to have a life of her own someday soon. That was the only thing about Dar that had ever made Lumi sad. Knowing Dar would be leaving for her own adventures without her.

Lumi had pinched and saved every penny she could for this day. She had dreamt of it many times: this day. The day she and Dar would take this adventure together. The adventure that would lead Dar to her life's calling... finding Famous.

She had so many questions about Famous and why Dar needed to find it or them. In her dreams this Famous appeared as a person, yet famous is not a name of any person she knew of. It must signify something, but what? And how will she help Dar find it?

Dar stood staring at the map. Her finger ran across the holes in the map where darts had once been. The holes had covered countries in and surrounding the UK, Ireland, and The Isle of Man. "I think we should definitely start here."

Chapter Three – Who Was That?

With only backpacks in hand, they set out on their journey. The thing about being a traveler is you go and figure out the rest on the way. Often times, you can spend days switching from a bus to a plane or train. This journey would be no different.

Rain fell from the sky as Dar looked out the window anxiously waiting for her mom to finish her checklist, a mundane task to Dar. She fidgeted as she watched the clouds appear darker by the second. Lumi went through the usual motions preparing to leave for an undetermined amount of time. She announced as she checked off every box, the windows are locked, mail is stopped… her voice barely audible to Dar.

Dar had been lost in thought. This trip was different, and she knew it. This was about her and her future. She felt anxious about it, unlike the many trips her and her mother had gone on before. Lumi snatched up her backpack and called Dar from her thoughts. "Time to go!"

They headed out the door. The rain had slowed to a mist. The walk was short to the bus stop. Dar made small talk about the weather to keep herself from overthinking about the days ahead. They would take the bus to a stop near the train station. They'd catch the train to the city, and then take the metro to get to the airport.

They had done this trip many times over the years and to Dar, today seemed no different than the other times. It was different and Lumi knew it, but she didn't know why she had this feeling of unease. She searched her surroundings several times, wondering who or what she expected to see. There was nothing unusual. People passed by as they got on or off the bus.

Sitting in the train station, Dar noticed Lumi seemed distracted. She was about to mention it when an older woman sat next to Lumi. They woman began talking to her like they were old friends, but Dar didn't recognize her. She couldn't hear the conversation so she leaned closer hoping to hear what the woman was saying. Dar tugged on Lumi's sleeve, but Lumi brushed her off. A screeching noise startled Dar. She looked away for only a second and when she turned back, the woman was gone. "Who was that?"

"Just someone asking about directions. It was nothing." Lumi's voice was nonchalant. Dar looked unconvinced, but the voice over the loudspeaker announced their train.

The trip to the airport was short and they found themselves waiting in the international flight's terminal. Lumi had gotten tickets to

Dublin. They could easily flights, trains, and ferries to the UK and the Isle of Man.

Dar started asking questions about the old woman. Lumi didn't have any answers, and she played like it was just a random conversation with a stranger. Dar eventually accepted it and moved on. "So where do you think our travels will find us this time? You usually have a plan of where we're going. Have you come up with one for this special trip?"

Lumi shook her head. The airline began boarding. The plane was only half full, so they moved up during the flight to be closer to the front of the plane. There was a movie playing, but both fell asleep during the flight. Lumi had dreams of a book, leather bound and slightly worn, floating in the air above a table of knickknacks. She looked around to see if she could figure out where she was. There were loads of tables and people milling about. She heard a voice saying "Dar's future is here."

It seemed like only minutes had gone by when Lumi was awakened by the flight attendant asking her to put her seat in the upright position. Dar was still fast asleep, so Lumi woke her and told her to get ready for landing. As always, Dar stared out the window, taking in the scenery with excitement.

She wondered what their new adventure would be. Dar knew this trip would be their most adventurous trip yet. They were flying by the seat of their pants. There were no carefully planned hotels or itineraries scheduled.

Upon landing, Dar and Lumi went through the normalcies of clearing customs and exited the airport to find a taxi into the city center.

"I guess we'll start by finding a hotel or a hostel for the night and make plans on looking into flea markets in the local area," Lumi said as they were leaving the airport. They quickly found a taxi and directed the driver to drop them off in the city center.

Lumi, deep in thought as they rode in the back of the taxi, was started at the sound of Dar's voice. "I'm starved," Dar said. Lumi asked the driver to drop them at a small café near the city center and he obliged.

The café was quaint and quiet. They sat at a table and chatted about the décor until a waitress appeared. Lumi asked if there was a telephone directory that she could look at and the waitress said she would bring one to her in just a few minutes.

As they ate, Lumi sat and listened as Dar prattled on about seeing some of the sites in Dublin before they left. The waitress came back with the telephone directory and Lumi went to work finding a hostel nearby. The waitress noticed that Lumi had the directory opened to hotels and she immediately asked if they were looking for a place to stay. Lumi said yes and asked if she had any low-cost recommendations. She smiled and pointed out the window at the street sign telling her to follow it a few blocks and there was a hostel on the right.

After paying for their lunch, they found their way to the hostel and checked in for two nights. Lumi had gotten a private room furnished with only two beds, a small table with two chairs, and a wardrobe. It was only a couple more dollars than the shared rooms with bunks, but they could then leave their backpacks and not have to drag them around town the next day.

"How are we going to find flea market?" Dar asked Lumi as they walked to their room.

"We will ask around, just like we usually do. This is just like any other adventure, Dar. We're looking for a treasure," Lumi beamed excitedly. "We're going to see where the road takes us. We'll find the way."

Dar pulled out a deck of cards and challenged Lumi to a game of gin. After an hour of playing cards, the jetlag set in and they found themselves calling it a night. After the lights were off, Dar started asking questions about the old woman at the train station again.

"Dar it's like I told you – just a random stranger asking for directions." Lumi's voice was more stern than she meant it to be.

"Well, she didn't seem random, and she disappeared into nowhere," Dar replied.

"Don't be silly. Now, get some sleep."

Dar started to protest as she yawned, mumbled a few other inaudible words, but soon, she drifted off to sleep.

Dar woke and saw that her mother's bed was empty. She got out of the bed and stretched.

Her mother came in the door with a towel on her head and some donuts in her hand.

"I didn't realize you could find donuts in the shower," Dar giggled as she stuffed one in her mouth. Lumi her a look and rolled her eyes with a smile on her face.

"Oh, guess what?" Lumi asked.

"Hmm?"

"I found a Farmers market close by, so when you're ready, we will start there. Then, we can check out Dublin, the castle, the library, and…" Lumi looked at Dar and could see the big smile on Dar's face. "What?"

"You are so cool, mom. Every time we go somewhere, you are ready to take on the city with such ambitious excitement. You make everything fun. I was just thinking how lucky I am, that's all."

Lumi's eyes were misty as she grabbed Dar and pulled her in for a hug. "Did I ever tell you that you are the best daughter in the whole wide world?"

"Yes, all the time. Hey, speaking of being a daughter, do you think we can see dad at some point on this trip?"

"Possibly. We'll play it by ear. It makes sense since we are on this side of the pond. Did you want a shower?"

"Nah, I'll take one when we get back."

Dar got dressed, grabbed her wallet, shoved it in the inside pocket of her coat with her passport, and was ready to go.

Chapter Four - The First Farmer's Market

Lumi and Dar decided to walk the mile to the farmers market, talking about the landmarks and shops they saw along the way. Lumi mentioned that the farmer's market had a lot of fruit and vegetables, but was expected to have tables set up with a garage-sale-type of stuff.

"One question," Dar interrupted. "How will we know when we find what we're looking for?"

Lumi stopped and looked at Dar. "Great question, and the answer is… I don't know. But we just will, I suppose. We've always found what we're looking for, right?" Lumi resumed walking.

"Yeah, but we normally know what we're looking for." Dar chuckled as the words came out of her mouth.

"We'll just have to figure it out, won't we."

Lumi pointed ahead of them. Dar turned around. There must have been fifty tables set up. It was a dreamlike setting – a field surrounded by beautiful greenery, a picturesque backdrop of trees and cottages in the distance. People were milling about, the tables shaded by colorful umbrellas and filled with fruit and bits of everything.

The blue sky was filled with fluffy white clouds, but dark clouds loomed in the distance. "We are probably going to get rained on," Lumi said as she pointed to the sky in the distance. They walked along picking up odds and ends, inspecting them and moving on to the next table.

Suddenly, Dar grabbed her mom's arm and pointed. "Isn't that the old woman from the train station?" she whispered and stared with wide eyes.

Lumi turned to look but didn't see the old woman. "Where?" She looked around. "Wait, the train station in New York? Don't be silly!"

"Look, over there. C'mon." Dar dragged her in the direction she had seen the woman go. "Where did she go?" Dar wondered aloud as she continued to pursue the woman.

They came to the end of the row of tables.
Dar looked in all directions, but could not see
the old woman anywhere. A nagging feeling
made Dar turn back to the last table. "Excuse
me, did you happen to see an older woman
come by a few seconds ago?" she asked the
girl at the table.

The girl looked up from the book she was
reading and replied in a strong Irish accent,
"I'm sorry, I wasn't looking." She set her
book down and stood up. "You look like
you're looking for something special." She
pointed at the things on her table behind her.
"I have some very special items here. Might
be what you are looking for."

Lumi and Dar walked around to the table in
the back noting the odd cards, amulets,
candles, and potions. Something caught Dar's
eye. It was a round charm on a tarnished

looking chain. It was glowing. "Mom, do you see that?"

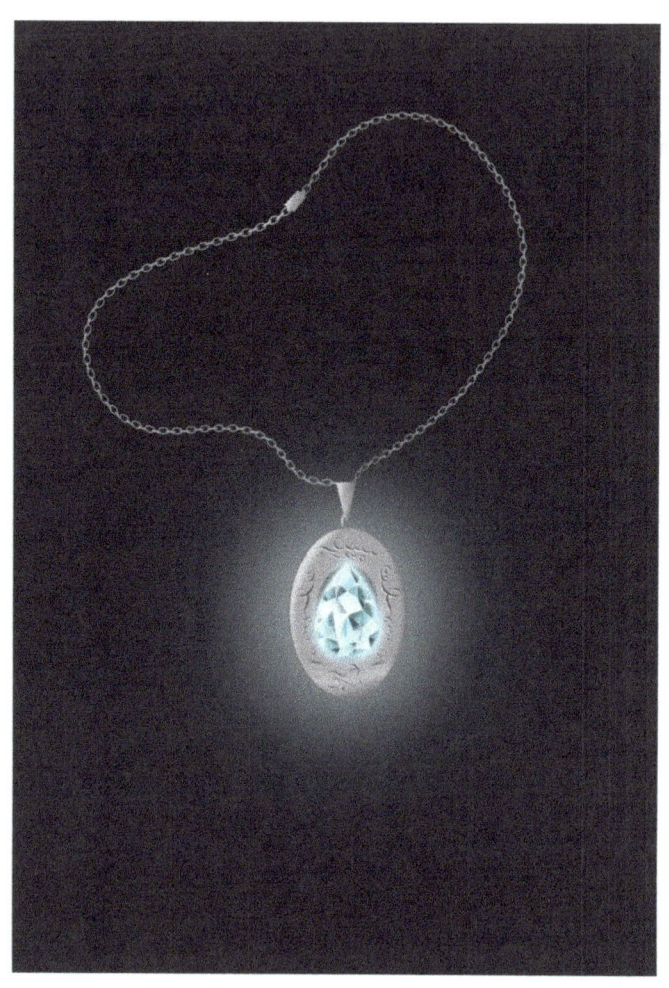

Lumi glanced over and shrugged. Dar looked back and it was no longer glowing. She picked it up. "I don't understand. It was glowing. I know it was glowing. Do you think this is what we're looking for?"

Lumi took it and held it in her hand and closed her eyes to concentrate. "I'm sorry, but don't think so."

The girl looked at Dar. "Take it!" she said. "Go ahead. It seems to belong to you."

Dar stepped back thinking that was an odd thing to say. "What do you mean?"

"You said it was glowing, so it must be yours. Go ahead, put it on." Dar was reluctant and stared at girl. The girl urged her again and Dar began to feel a little uncomfortable.

She set the amulet back on the table. "I don't know," Dar said. "I'll think about it. Thank you."

"No, seriously. You may have it, no charge. It's yours," the girl insisted. She picked it up off the table, opened the clasp, and walked toward Dar. Lumi stepped between them protectively. "It won't hurt you," the girl said. "I'm sorry if I'm making you nervous. It's a special charm. It's for protection and it's chosen you to protect." The girl stepped forward toward Dar again. Dar looked at Lumi questionably and shrugged as if she was asking for her opinion. "It's a magical charm," the girl continued. "There's a myth about this charm, that it empowers the person that wears it, but it only glows for someone with powers to be empowered. I'm sure it sounds crazy to you, not being from here, but trust me, it only glows for the one it belongs to. Somewhere in your past, it was in your family, and now it has found its way back to your family. Please take it."

Lumi appeared to give her blessing and moved out from between the two. The girl clasped it around Dar's neck. Dar thought she felt a strange sensation flow through her, but then remembered her overactive imagination. Drops of rain fell from the sky as Dar and Lumi looked at the charm. They turned to thank the girl, but she was gone, table and all.

"That's creepy," Dar said to her mom.

"Yeah, creepy," Lumi agreed.

"Should I take it off?" she asked, as lightning flashed and thunder roared. Huge drops began to downpour from the sky. They ran towards the trees, ducked under one, and watched as people packed their stuff into boxes and took down their tables. They huddled together waiting for the rain to lighten up, cold and wet, knowing it was a bit of a walk back to the hostel.

Time passed slowly and soon they were the only ones remaining. The dark sky seemed to lighten, and the rain slowed to a drizzle, then to a sprinkle when they emerged from the cover of the tree. They sloshed their way out of the field and back to the road.

Chapter Five - The "Awake" Dream

The sun appeared from the clouds making steam rise from the road. Dar and Lumi were walking back to the hostel in silence.

"Seriously, that was weird, right?" Dar was the first to speak. "I mean, there was no way she could have packed up and left in just a few seconds. It was like we imagined the whole thing, but look…" She grasped the charm and held it in her hand. She hadn't noticed the small crystal in the center that now glistened different colors – purple, blue, then red – from the sun as she moved her hand. Then a thought crossed her mind. Perhaps it hadn't glowed at all, perhaps it was just the sun bouncing off it. She quickly told Lumi of her new theory.

"Well, at least once we clean it up a bit, it will be quite pretty. I must admit I was a little nervous about that girl. How silly is that?" Lumi laughed at herself.

Dar laughed with her and said, "Me too!" She exaggerated the words causing them both to laugh harder. "We are so ridiculous, like what was she going to do, strangle me with a necklace?" They laughed and laughed at how silly they thought they had been.

Trudging along laughing and dodging puddles, Dar's stomach growled loudly, causing another fit of laughter. "Hungry? Are you ready for lunch?" Lumi asked.

"Definitely, I'm starved!" Dar answered.

"Obviously." Lumi smiled and thought about all of these moments. The moments people miss or take advantage of. Not her. She cherished every moment with Dar.

They walked for another fifteen minutes before coming to a small brick building with a glass door. In front of the building was a chalkboard sign with bubbly letters that read *Today's special: Fish and chips.*

Dar and Lumi read the sign and began crossing the street toward the restaurant. A car came from nowhere and splashed through a puddle, dousing them with muddy water. A young girl about Dar's age came running from the restaurant with a dish towel.

"I saw from the window," said the girl. "You poor dears! Here, come, dry off." She ushered them into the restaurant. Patrons looked up and glanced at them, then continued eating their lunch. "It's just terrible that they couldn't be bothered to slow down." Her thick Irish accent was sweet and charming.

Dar and Lumi sat at a table. The waitress gasped when she saw the charm dangling around Dar's neck when she leaned forward to remove her jacket.

"Is everything okay?" Dar asked.

The waitress smiled and nodded as she quickly walked away. A moment later, the waitress reappeared with menus and two glasses of water. They refused the menus and said they would be having the special. Staring at the charm around Dar's neck, the waitress smiled and nodded. As she walked away, Dar whispered to Lumi, "Did you see how she reacted when she saw this charm?"

"Yeah, weird, huh? Maybe you should ask her about it," Lumi said cryptically, raising her eyebrows.

Bells chimed as the door to the restaurant opened. Dar, Lumi, and the other patrons glanced at the door as a woman walked in. The woman scurried past Dar and Lumi, glancing back at Dar before hurrying into the kitchen. Dar and Lumi gave each other puzzled looks.

The woman and the waitress came back to the table. The waitress spoke first. "My name is Destiny, and this is my auntie. Do you mind if we sit with you for a minute?" she asked.

Lumi waved her hand towards the chairs as she said, "Please do."

The women sat in silence for a moment giving off nervous energy.

"I noticed your necklace," Destiny started. "It's lovely. Where ever did you get it?"

Dar told the story of the morning they had. After she had finished, a man came from the kitchen with two plates of food. He set them down in front of Lumi and Dar, glancing at the ladies at the table, shaking his head, and walking away. With that, the ladies got up and excused themselves from the table. Lumi started to protest, but they waved her off as they walked back into the kitchen.

Dar shoved a French fry in her mouth. She was hungry and wasn't letting the strange goings on stop her from eating. Her mom watched her for a second before starting in on her own lunch. They were so hungry and the food tasted so good that they moaned with every bite. Every once in a while, they would glance at the door to the kitchen, both wondering if Destiny and her aunt would come back. Suddenly, the front door chimed again. The patrons glanced at the door, but there was no one there. There was only wind, a strong, insane amount of wind that blew the door wide open. The wild wind blew chairs and tables over. The lights went out. The room grew dark… as dark as night.

Lumi couldn't see Dar. She reached out in search of her. "Dar?" she called. No one answered. She called for Dar repeatedly. Still, no answer was heard. Panic-stricken and screaming for her child, she grasped at the air, trying to find Dar in the darkness.

Then, as fast as it started... it was over. The room was light again. The wind had stopped. The restaurant appeared as though nothing had happened. Dar was in front of her chatting along about going to other flea markets, or maybe even going to London. Lumi sat staring at her, in shock. Nothing was out of place. Nothing had happened. Dar noticed her mom's bewildered look. "Mom? You, ok? You look pale."

Lumi glanced around the restaurant. "It was a dream," she whispered, barely audible. Confused and panicked, Lumi yelled, "We need to go! We need to go NOW!" She immediately stood, searching for the waitress to pay for their lunch.

At the sound of her yelling, Destiny came out of the kitchen. Lumi explained that she needed the check right away. Destiny tried to calm Lumi in hopes the duo might stay so they could talk more. Lumi wouldn't be calmed. She handed Destiny enough Euros to cover the food, grabbed Dar's hand, and dragged her daughter out the door.

"What's going on? What happened?" Dar asked wildly. She was struggling to understand what was wrong but followed her mom down the road. "Mom, wait! What is going on?"

"I don't know, but we need to put some distance between us and that place. I had a dream," Lumi explained.

"A dream? But you were awake the whole time. I saw you. What do you mean? You were awake, right?"

"Yes, and I don't know what it means. I've never had an 'awake' dream."

Chapter Six - The Knock

Dar and Lumi's walk back to the hostel was quiet, Lumi lost in thought and Dar in quiet contemplation of what to do next.

"I think we're going to leave Dublin tomorrow," Lumi announced as she shut the door to their room.

"Can we talk about what happened?" Dar asked.

Lumi paced the room a few times before she spoke. "It was really eerie… downright scary, even. There was a wind… darkness… and I couldn't find you. Then, I looked up and you were there, and none of it had happened. You know, I just freaked out that it was a premonition or something. I'm sorry if I scared you, sweetie. I'm wondering if Dublin was a bad idea."

Dar put her arms around Lumi. "That must have been so scary. Well, I'm here and we're okay. That's what is important." Dar could see that her mom was struggling. "Maybe you're right," Dar continued. "Dublin isn't the place. There really aren't too many markets here anyway. I've been thinking about this and was wondering if you remember anything else about your dreams from home. I mean, a market with lots of tables full of bits. Maybe if you concentrate on that and meditate or something…"

Lumi chuckled. "It doesn't really work like that."

A hard knock on the door startled them both. Slowly and reluctantly, they walked to the door together. "Who is it?" Lumi demanded, trying to sound more confident and less fearful. No one answered. Upon opening the door, they were surprised to see only an envelope on the floor. Lumi looked into the hallway hoping to see the person who left it, but the hallway was empty.

"Well, I wonder who this is from," Lumi said as she picked up the envelope. She opened the envelope and in bold read the words:

Follow the map, use the compass.

"What map? What compass?" Lumi wondered aloud.

follow the map.
Use the compass.

"Who knows? I don't trust this." Dar grabbed the note, crumpled it up, and tossed it in the trash bin. "I'm thinking it's a good idea to explore other options… like we always do when we're looking for something. Let's write down all the info we have and go from there."

Lumi didn't answer right away. She was weighing the options. "We don't have much to go on. Maybe we should go back and talk to the two women at the fish and chips place."

"No way! Are you crazy? What if that was a premonition and what you saw actually happens? I say we stay far away from there."

"Valid point, but…" Lumi was pacing the room. She pulled the crumpled paper from the bin, inspected it again, and set it on the table. "So, what do we know?" Lumi wondered aloud. "We know that when we were throwing the darts, they kept pointing us to come here. After getting here, we went to a flea market and you found a pendant and… wait… the pendant… maybe that's got something to do with the compass or the map. Let me take a look at that thing."

Dar took the necklace off and handed it to Lumi she inspected it and found that there was significant tarnish on the back. It appeared to have something engraved on it. Could it be the map?

"How did we not notice this before?" Lumi asked as she pointed out the engraving.

"Well, that's pretty easy. Let's see… there was the rain and then there was the car with puddles, which led us to the crazy people at the fish and chips restaurant causing your premonition. I mean, I think there's a lot of things that could possibly have detoured us from actually checking the necklace out. I didn't even mention the vanishing table at the farmer's market." Lumi rolled her eyes at her daughter's sarcastic reply.

"We have to clean this up a bit," Lumi remarked as she went to her backpack to get toothpaste and a cloth. She began rubbing the tarnish from the back of the pendant. "Look!" She handed the pendant to Dar.

The back of the pendant revealed a map. Dar examined it, then, flipped it over and ran her thumb over the stone in the middle of the front of it. It seemed to come to life. A flicker of light emanated from the stone. "Did you see that?" Dar whispered in amazement. She ran her thumb across it and again it flickered. The stone began to glow brighter the more she touched it. Dar held the pendant in the palm of her hand, an intense blue glow shining brightly from it. "Strange… so here's the map. Where's the compass?"

"Good question."

Chapter Seven – The Compass

Dar clasped the chain back around her neck. She grabbed the paper from the table and read it again. "We must have the compass and not know it," she reasoned. "I mean, look at this note. Whoever left it knows we have the pendant. We must be missing something. Hmm…" Dar flipped the note over looking for clues and held it up to the light. "What are we missing?"

"It has to be something to do with that pendant, right?" Lumi walked over and looked closer at the pendant.

"Do you want me to take it off again?" Dar reached back to the clasp.

"No, that's okay. We don't want to risk dropping it and losing it before we figure this out. We're definitely missing something, but what?" Lumi sat down on the edge of the bed and thought for a moment. "Let's try something." Lumi got up, walked to the light switch, and turned it off. "Rub that pendant again."

Dar pinched the pendant between her thumb and index finger and rubbed the pendant for several seconds. The light grew brighter and brighter. She kept rubbing the pendant until, suddenly, the back slid sideways. "Whoa…" Dar remarked.

"What? What happened?" Lumi moved closer to Dar and could see that the pendant had a hidden compartment. Inside the compartment was the most unusual looking compass.

"Looks like we've found the compass." Dar sat on the bed and took the piece out of the pendant. Lumi sat next to her and Dar set the pieces between them on the bed. The way each piece was shaped, they knew they fit together somehow. After several minutes of trying to piece it together, they finally got it. Dar clicked the pieces together and the arm on the compass began to rotate in circles rapidly. Dar placed it in the palm of her hand. Dar and Lumi stared intently as the arm slowed to a stop.

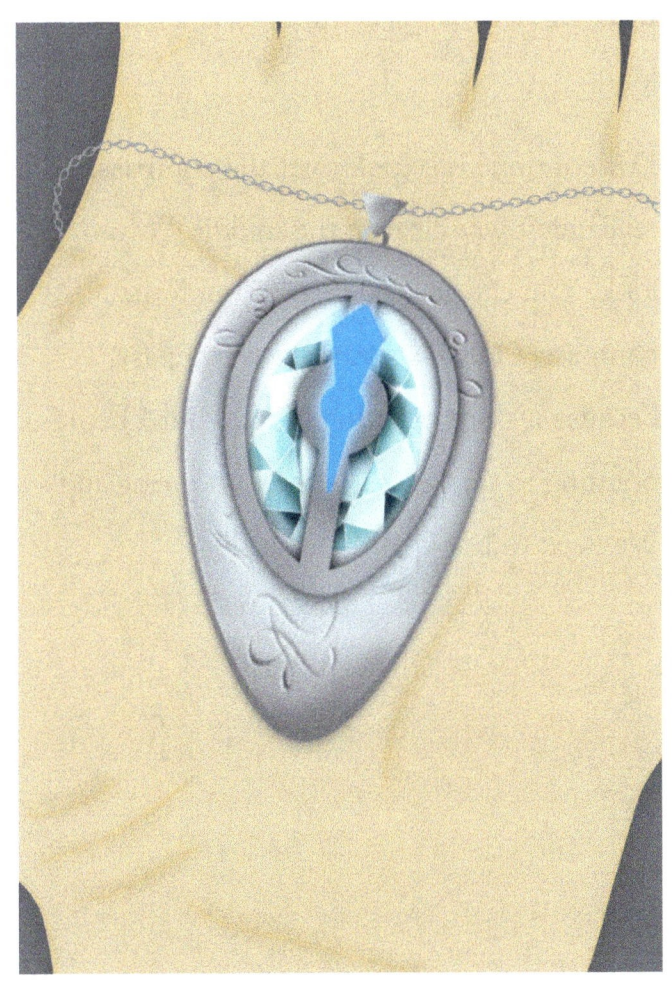

"Well, it looks like we need to go that way... wherever that way is," Lumi finally said out loud.

Dar continued to look over the compass, realizing it was clear in the middle. "Mom, look. You can see the map through the compass. Only it's not really a compass, because it's not pointing North. But I bet it's pointing to our next destination... England! We need to book some tickets!"

Chapter Eight – The Cheapest Option

After the big discovery, Lumi and Dar were excited to start planning for their next stop. England was, for the most part, only separated by water, so there were plenty of travel options for them to choose from. Dar and Lumi went to the front desk of the hostel for information. Lumi grabbed several brochures of local attractions and restaurants.

"I think it's about time to get some dinner, what do you think?" Lumi asked as she held up a brochure with a picture of a bowl of Irish stew on the front.

"Looks good," Dar replied, salivating.

The place was nearby so they decided to walk. They were seated promptly and ordered the stew. While they waited for their dinner, they looked at other brochures of the local festivities and attractions. Dar came across a brochure of a ferry they could take to get to the UK and showed her mom. "This might be a fun way to get where were going."

Lumi looked at it and the prices. "And it may be the cheapest option, too. We should save money whenever we can. We don't know how long or how far we'll be travelling."

The server arrived with their stew. Lumi smiled as she looked up at her waitress, a young girl wearing a traditional Irish green and white dress that laced up the front.

"Be careful it's hot," the waitress warned. Her accent was thick as she spoke. "Are you thinking about taking the ferry? It's a beautiful trip across. There are several that run every day."

After paying and thanking the girl for her service, Dar and Lumi started walking back toward hostel. It was a beautiful night, the streets dimly lit by street lanterns. Suddenly, the street began to darken. Dar froze as the world faded to black. Then, just as suddenly as the darkness came, the dust cleared.

"What just happened?" Dar screamed looking around. She was no longer in the street. Instead, she stood in a small, strange shop. She could see something glowing on one of the tables, but couldn't tell what it was. As she tried to get closer, the shop began to blur. She was trying to focus and when the darkness came again. "Mom?" Dar called, reaching for her mother. With that, the world came back into focus. She was back on the street quietly walking alongside her mother.

"What was that?" Dar yelled.

Lumi saw the streetlights flicker. "It's okay, sweetie," Lumi reassured Dar. "Those streetlights are probably just old and need new bulbs."

"No, mom! Not the streetlights. I just had something happen… something weird." As they made their way to the hostel, Dar told her of her strange experience.

"Hmm… it sounds like you had a vision like I had at the restaurant. Are you sure it was a shop and not a flea market?"

Dar closed her eyes and tried to remember the details of her premonition. "It was definitely a shop. I think it was full of used stuff. It didn't look all shiny and new… it looked kind of junky."

"A charity shop?" Lumi asked excitedly.

"A what?"

"Basically, a thrift store. Perhaps I was wrong about the flea market. Maybe… well, no… because you found the necklace at the flea market. This is your first dream, but you're awake. This is incredible! When we get to England, we'll look for your shop. Hurry, let's get inside and get ourselves ready to leave early tomorrow morning."

With that, Dar and Lumi arrived at their hostel, went to their room, and got ready for bed. Both were too excited to sleep. They couldn't wait to get on the road again. Dar tossed and turned, but eventually, sleep found her.

Chapter Nine - The Ferry

The train pulled away from the station. Dar looked around. She couldn't quite figure out how she got there. A voice whispered, "You must find the baby... your baby. She needs a mother... she needs you..."

"I don't understand!" Dar called out frantically looking for the person she heard whispering.

"Dar?" Lumi jumped from her bed and ran to Dar. "Dar, wake up. Dar, you're dreaming." Lumi shook Dar's shoulders and Dar slowly opened her eyes.

"It was so real, I…" Dar's voice faded as she leaned her head on Lumi's shoulder.

"What was your dream about?"

Dar lifted her head and began to speak. "It was confusing… very confusing." She told her everything she remembered from her dream.

Her mother smiled. "I can't believe you're finally dreaming with meaning, and it's obviously a sign."

"A sign? A sign of what?"

"Your destiny, my sweet girl. Well, since we are up, let's get ready for our ferry ride." Lumi's smile radiated. She jumped up and clapped her hands. "This is going to be fun!"

Lumi and Dar showered and put their stuff together while chatting about Dar's dream and all the possible meanings.

They arrived early at the ferry port. Lumi thought she saw the girl from the fish-and-chips restaurant, but when she looked again, the girl was gone. Several people joined them in line to get on the ferry. They listened to the chatter around them.

The ferry was a little crowded, but they found their way to a place at the railing to watch as they left the dock. It was a beautiful day and the water was mostly smooth. The ferry ride took about five hours to get to the port on the other side. To kill time, they walked around the ferry eating snacks and watching with excitement as the land in the distance seemed to grow bigger and bigger. The greenery looked absolutely magical in the bright sunshine and they couldn't wait to get on shore.

"I always get super excited when we go to a new place. What do you think is on the other side?" Dar asked.

"It is exciting, isn't it?" Lumi looked past Dar as she said it. She could swear she saw that girl again.

Dar looked turned and looked in the direction Lumi had been staring. "Everything okay?"

Lumi nodded. "It's just…" she glanced again. "Nothing… never mind." She waved it off.

They watched as the ferry docked and the lines were safely looped around the cleats. They disembarked the ferry and walked through the customs area. The town was small but bustling with people. They found their way to a small café to order lunch.

Chapter Ten – The Journal

"I think we should do some site-seeing and maybe some shopping," Lumi said.

"Maybe we will find a charity shop," Dar replied enthusiastically.

"Maybe… but today is about the journey… our adventure. Let's just see where the day takes us."

Dar and Lumi walked through a maritime museum, a famous church, and along the beach. When they were sure they'd seen all they could see for the day, they found a quaint little inn not far from the ferry port and booked a room for the night. The inn had a cruise theme, with rooms named and decorated like cabins on a ship. Their room looked out to the sea, the windows like portholes. Lumi watched as Dar stared out to the sea.

Lumi knew they were close to finding whatever it was they were looking for, and their adventure was coming to an end.

Dar turned. "What do you want to do now?" she asked. "Go for a walk, grab dinner, play cards… thoughts?"

"Yes, to all of that!" Lumi laughed. Lumi grabbed her jacket. "Let's go!"

The streets were filled with tourists shopping and enjoying chatter. They watched the beach filled with children flying kites. Lumi felt a tug on her arm but when she looked back there was no one there. She looked all around and could not see her daughter. Lumi called her name several times.

Dar could hear Lumi calling her name, but she was mesmerized by a sign that said "Charity Shop" at the end of the street. The dream came to her once again. She stood in the dimly lit shop with tables of odds and ends and racks of clothes hanging. A table had something glowing. The scene was familiar.

"Dar!" Lumi grabbed her arm, bringing her out of her state. "You scared me half to death! I…" Lumi stopped and looked in the direction Dar was looking. "Is that the shop from your dream?"

"I don't know," Dar whispered.

Lumi grabbed her hand and pulled her toward the shop. "Let's go and see, shall we?"

Dar felt nervous as she walked with her mom along the street, down the block to the shop. She tugged on the door handle, but the door was locked. They peered in the window to an empty store and Dar shook her head. "It's not the one."

A passerby told them that the shop had moved a couple streets over and gave them directions. They walked the few short blocks to the shop. Dar could feel a knot in her stomach as they reached the door.

Lumi held the door open as Dar slowly walked in. The shop was bright and colorful, unlike in her dream. At first, she didn't see anything, but then a bright glow from one of the tables caught her attention.

"Do you see that?" she whispered to Lumi as she pointed to the table.

"What?" Lumi replied.

"There's something on that table… it's glowing!"

Lumi looked but saw nothing.

She walked to the table wondering if she was awake or dreaming again, but there it was glowing, and she reached for it. The object on the table that was glowing so brightly she could not see what it was at first. She picked it up and realized it was a journal. Upon holding it, she immediately could see a vision of a child. Her child. A child that needed a mother. It all became clear. She flipped open to the first page. It held only a few words: Journal the journey and she will follow your path. Dar flipped through the pages looking for more, but they all appeared blank. As she flipped through the journal, her mind was filled with images of a trek to find the child.

Alexis Anicque's Author Pages

Amazon Author

Goodreads Author

Author Website

Alexis Anicque's Social Media

Facebook

Instagram

Twitter

LinkedIn

Authors Buying Books Facebook Group

First Chapter on YouTube

Famous' adventure began with fairytales of monsters, witches and wizards. The fairytales her mother had told her as a child, were not just fairy tales, but a world of magic and danger where she not only finds out where she came from, but who she is.

The adventure continues as Famous' quest to find out more about her family she must set out for another journey to solve the mystery of The Monster in The Forest.

This fun and heartfelt Christmas story starts with a touch of adventure and a bit of magic and leaves you with the perfect pumpkin bread recipe to create your own famous Christmas memories.

About The Author

Alexis Ancique is an experienced author and avid adventurer, driven by her love for travel and exploration. As a mother of two grown children and Nana of four, her family is her pride and joy. In her free time, she enjoys writing and sailing. Her insatiable wanderlust often finds her jumping on planes, trains, or buses to visit new places all over the world. Although she lives in a charming cottage in the woods, she's equally drawn to the energy and excitement of city life. Overall, she just loves adventure! She hopes to share that with you!

Alexis Anicque is the author of multiple genres in ebook, paperback, and audio.

Hardbacks available soon.

www.ingramcontent.com/pod-product-compliance
Lightning Source LLC
Chambersburg PA
CBHW060235180626
46813CB00007B/3099